THIS BOOK BELONGS TO

....

AUTUMN
PUBLISHING

Published in 2021
First published in the UK by Autumn Publishing
An imprint of Igloo Books Ltd, Cottage Farm, NN6 0BJ, UK
Owned by Bonnier Books, Sveavägen 56, Stockholm, Sweden
www.igloobooks.com
Autumn is an imprint of Bonnier Books UK

© 2021 Disney Enterprises, Inc.

0321 001
2 4 6 8 10 9 7 5 3 1
ISBN 978-1-80022-039-3
Printed and manufactured in China

From the Movie

DISNEY
RAYA
AND
THE LAST DRAGON

BOOK
OF THE
FILM

AUTUMN
PUBLISHING

Long ago, in a land called Kumandra, people lived peacefully alongside dragons.

But everything changed when a dark plague called the Druun arrived. They turned people to stone, multiplying and destroying all in their path. The dragons fought valiantly, but soon, only one remained. As legend was told, the last dragon poured magic into a gem and BOOMED the Druun away.

Then, all of the stone people
came back to life! But it was at a
cost – the last dragon disappeared,
never to be seen again. Without
dragons, humans lost their way and
Kumandra divided into five separate lands:
Tail, Talon, Spine, Heart and Fang.
The Dragon Gem remained in Heart,
hidden inside a secret chamber, where it
was guarded for centuries.

One night, a young warrior named Raya crept into Heart's ancient temple, determined to get to the Dragon Gem. With the help of her friend Tuk Tuk, she made it past hidden traps and into the secret chamber.

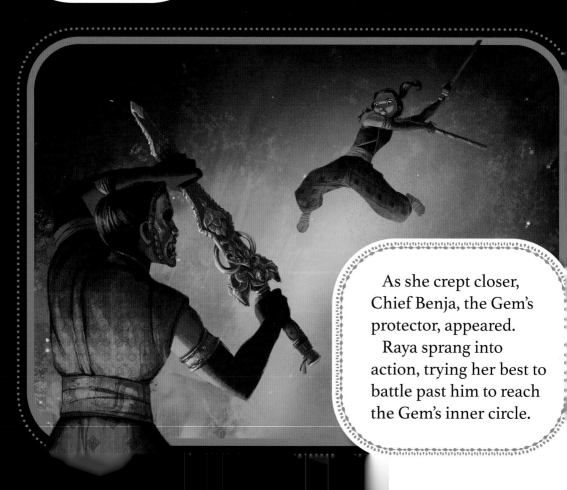

As she crept closer, Chief Benja, the Gem's protector, appeared. Raya sprang into action, trying her best to battle past him to reach the Gem's inner circle.

But Chief Benja disarmed her.

"BOOP," he said, tapping her nose. "You lost, Raya."

"Did I?" she asked.

He was surprised to see Raya's toe on the Gem's inner circle!

"Don't beat yourself up too much, Chief Benja," said Raya. "You gave it your best!"

"I won't," he said. "And it's either Father or Ba to you." He smiled. "You did good, dewdrop. You passed the test."

Raya took a deep breath and joined her father. The Gem was dazzling.

"Wow," she said. "The spirit of Sisu." Sisu was the name of the last dragon.

"For generations, our family has sworn to protect the Gem," Benja said. "Today, you will join that legacy."

He dipped his hands into the glittering pool that surrounded the Gem and gently poured water onto Raya's forehead. The glowing drops began to float around her as he completed the ceremony. "Raya, Princess of Heart, my daughter. You are now a Guardian of the Dragon Gem."

Benja told Raya he believed they could bring back Kumandra. "There's a reason why each land is named after a part of the dragon. We were once unified harmoniously as one," Benja said. He told Raya that someone just had to take the first step in uniting the lands once more.

Benja invited each of the lands to Heart to try and ease the tensions between their peoples. As he welcomed the guests, the chiefs were suspicious of his intentions.

Raya looked over the crowd, wondering how she could help to rebuild their trust.

Stood at the head of Fang's tribe was a young girl around Raya's age. Raya stepped forward and introduced herself.

"I'm Namaari," said the young girl. She was Fang's princess.

"Come on. Have you eaten yet?" said Raya, and the two girls crossed the bridge into Heart.

With tensions eased, everyone followed.

Raya was surprised to see that Namaari wore a Sisu necklace. She also showed Raya an ancient Fang scroll that said Sisu was sleeping at the end of a river. To Raya's surprise, Namaari gifted her necklace to her!

Raya smiled. "Come with me."

She led her new friend to the inner circle and the Dragon Gem. The two girls stood for a moment, fixed by its wonder. But then, Namaari knocked Raya down!

As the two battled, Fang soldiers appeared. Benja jumped in, landing beside Raya. Soon, armies from all the lands surrounded them.

As Benja tried to calm everyone, someone shot an arrow at him! Raya rushed to his side.

The armies fought over the Gem until finally... it shattered! There was a deafening BOOM as Druun emerged from a crack in the ground! Benja held one of the broken Gem pieces up and the Druun backed away. Realising the pieces still had magic, people from each kingdom scrambled for the remaining shards.

Druun continued to multiply as panic and chaos enveloped Heart.
Raya, her father and Tuk Tuk fled the city, but as they
reached the bridge, Druun closed in on them.
Benja gave Raya the broken Gem piece and
his sword.

"Don't give up on them," he said. "I love you,
my dewdrop." Then he pushed her and
Tuk Tuk off the bridge!

Raya fell towards the safety of the
water, where Druun could not go.
When she looked back, they had
turned her father to stone.

As the years passed, Raya dedicated herself to searching the world's rivers for Sisu. She hoped the dragon could once again boom the Druun away, and bring her father back.

With Tuk Tuk and her father's sword at her side, she finally reached the last river.

She walked along the water to an old ship. "Six years of searching and we end up at a literal shipwreck," Raya said. "That's not a bad sign, is it?"

Tuk Tuk grunted.

Raya headed inside the ship's remains and found the river's end, a trickle of water that stopped at a wall of rock.

Repeating the offering she had made at every river before, Raya asked for Sisu's help. Then she waited patiently.

But this time, something different happened. Drops of water swirled around and formed... SISU!

"Is that food?" the dragon said, digging into Raya's bag. "I was so focused on booming away the Druun, I forgot to have breakfast today."

Sisu didn't realise that hundreds of years had passed since the Druun were last defeated! Raya explained that she needed her to boom the Druun away... again.

Sisu said she could do it, but she needed the Dragon Gem.

"YOU BROKE IT?" she shouted when Raya told her the bad news.

Raya suggested she make another one.

"I'm going to be real with you, alright? I'm not, like, the best dragon," Sisu said. She confessed that it was the magic of other dragons that made the Gem, not hers.

But when Sisu touched Raya's Gem piece, she began to glow. The two realised the magic might work, if they collected the pieces from each land.

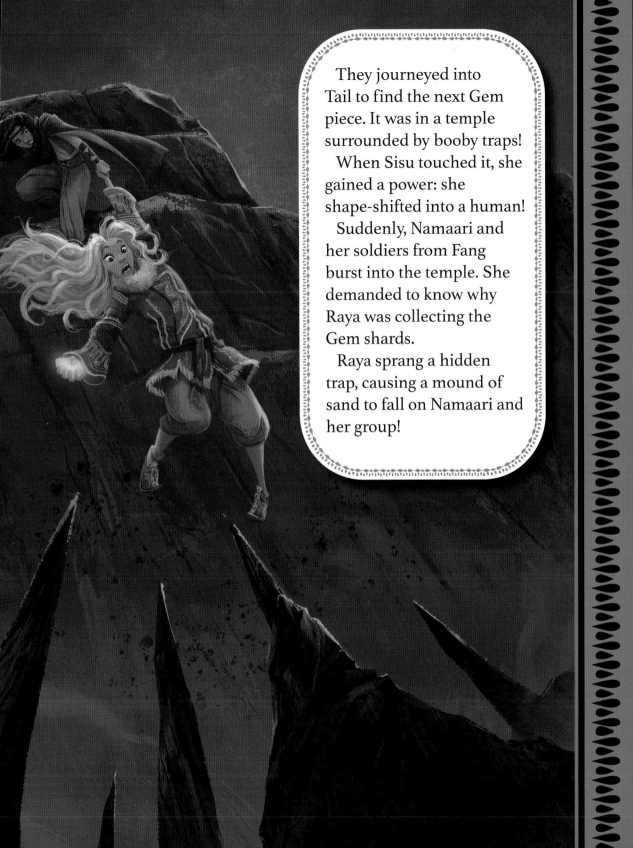

They journeyed into
Tail to find the next Gem
piece. It was in a temple
surrounded by booby traps!

When Sisu touched it, she
gained a power: she
shape-shifted into a human!

Suddenly, Namaari and
her soldiers from Fang
burst into the temple. She
demanded to know why
Raya was collecting the
Gem shards.

Raya sprang a hidden
trap, causing a mound of
sand to fall on Namaari and
her group!

Raya and Sisu managed to escape from the temple, racing away on Tuk Tuk. Namaari and her soldiers followed closely behind.

Reaching the docks, Raya, Sisu and Tuk Tuk hopped onto a shrimp boat where a boy named Boun appeared, ready to take their order.

"Welcome to the world-famous Shrimp-orium!"

Raya convinced Boun to sail towards Talon – promising him some jade as payment.

As they sailed further away from Namaari, Raya and Sisu began to relax a little.

"Okay, who's hungry?" Boun asked as he served Sisu and Raya bowls of congee.

"It could be poisoned," Raya whispered to Sisu. But Sisu gulped down the congee.

"This is delicious! By the way... NOT... poison!"

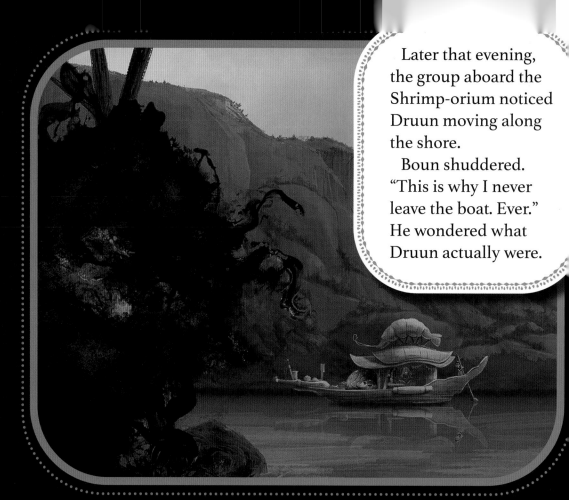

Later that evening, the group aboard the Shrimp-orium noticed Druun moving along the shore.

Boun shuddered. "This is why I never leave the boat. Ever." He wondered what Druun actually were.

"They're like a relentless fire that consumes everything," Sisu said, "until there's nothing left."

The group imagined what the world would be like without Druun as they continued sailing towards Talon.

When they arrived, Raya asked Sisu to stay on the boat. Then, she and Tuk Tuk set out to find Talon's Gem shard. But, on the way there, a crying baby distracted Raya and three Ongis stole the Gem pieces from Raya's bag!

"Really? A con-baby!" said Raya in disbelief.

She and Tuk Tuk chased down the baby and the Ongis to get the pieces back.

Meanwhile, Sisu, who wanted to help Raya by getting the Talon Chief a gift, was getting into trouble with the merchants in the marketplace for taking things.

She didn't have any money, and she didn't know how payment worked.

An old lady heard Sisu mention the Dragon Gem pieces and came to her rescue.

"Get away from her!" yelled the old lady to the merchants before turning to Sisu. "Come, dear. Don't be afraid."

The old lady led Sisu outside the city gates. A Druun emerged and she held up Talon's Gem piece! "Now, you're going to tell me where I can find those other Dragon Gem pieces," she said. "Or, I'll have to leave you outside with that... thing!"

Sisu was shocked. "But I trusted you!"
"Big mistake," said the old lady, backing away.
As the Druun closed in, Raya sped in on Tuk Tuk, grabbed Sisu, and snatched up the Talon Gem piece!
Sisu gained another power: fog. The thick fog scared away the Druun and gave Raya, Sisu and Tuk Tuk the cover they needed to escape.

"Sisu, I told you to stay on the boat!" Raya shouted as the pair rode Tuk Tuk onto the boat where Boun was serving food to the baby and Ongis.

"Thanks for the new customers!" he said, grinning.

"Yeah, I sorta promised to buy them all the congee they could eat," said Raya.

"Well, we're stuck with them now," said Boun. "Because Ongis have nine stomachs."

As they sailed away from Talon, Raya warned Sisu about strangers. "The world's broken, you can't trust anyone."

"Or maybe the world's broken BECAUSE you don't trust anyone," said Sisu.

As they reached Spine, Sisu charged ahead, carrying a pot of soup. She was determined to show Raya that people weren't all bad. Raya begged Sisu to stop, but Sisu carried on and the two were suddenly caught up in a trap.

Meanwhile, in the land of Fang, Namaari had returned and told her mother, Chief Virana, about Raya's efforts to collect all the Gem pieces. Namaari wanted the royal army to assist her in catching Raya so they could take the pieces for themselves.

Virana smiled proudly at her daughter. "Namaari, you've truly grown into the leader I raised you to be."

Back in Spine, Raya and Sisu were in a hut, tied up, and hanging from a giant tusk.

Suddenly, the door opened and a fierce warrior named Tong stepped in. "You two must be dung of brain to think you could steal Spine's Dragon Gem."

Moments later, Tuk Tuk burst through the door of Tong's hut. Boun, the baby and the Ongis tied the warrior up!

As Boun freed Sisu and Raya, he announced, "Fang's here."

Namaari stood outside the village gates and demanded that Raya come out.

Raya peered out of the window and saw that Spine was empty. She looked at Tong. "You're the only one here."

"My people battled the Druun with much valour... but lost," he said sadly.

Deciding to trust Tong, Raya came up with a plan. She would distract Namaari and her soldiers if Tong helped her friends escape.

Tong agreed and Raya cut him free.

Outside, Namaari was growing impatient. She turned to her soldiers. "Burn them out."

They aimed their flaming crossbows, but before they could fire, the gate swung open.

"Hey there, princess undercut, fancy meeting you here," said Raya.

Namaari cracked her knuckles. "You and those Dragon Gem pieces are coming with me."

Raya raised her sword and as the two began to battle, Tong led Sisu, Boun, the baby and Ongis out of the city unseen.

But when Sisu caught a glimpse of Raya defeated and lying on the ground, she couldn't walk away.

   As Namaari prepared for a final blow, a blast of fog stopped her.
Sisu emerged in her dragon form, stepping between Namaari
and Raya.
   All was still as everyone stood, speechless, staring in awe at Sisu.
"Yup. She's a dragon. Let's go. Go! Come on!" Raya urged her friends.
   Sisu gazed into Namaari's eyes before turning away and
disappearing into the forest. Raya and the group followed, heading
quickly back to the boat.

When the others learned what Raya and Sisu were trying to do, they committed to help. They had all lost people to the Druun. Tong handed Sisu Spine's Gem piece and, suddenly, it began to rain. They realised that Sisu had gained another power!

Now there was only Fang's Gem
piece left to find. Sisu wanted to make
Namaari an offering and ask for help,
but Raya thought it was impossible.

Sisu grabbed Raya and took to the sky,
running on raindrops towards Heart.

Sisu took Raya inside the ancient temple and told her how the Dragon Gem came to be... as Druun attacked, her siblings put all their magic into the Gem. Then, to her surprise, they gave it to her.

"All I know is I trusted them and they trusted me," she said. She believed it was their trust that changed her. And it was with that trust that she was able to rid the world of the Druun. "The same thing can happen with Namaari."

Raya wasn't convinced. She couldn't see how she could ever trust Namaari again.

"But if somehow you could, you wouldn't just bring your father back – you'd also bring back his dream... Kumandra," said Sisu.

Raya finally agreed to try. She said they would need a great gift and Raya knew just the thing – the dragon pendant that Namaari had given her as a child.

Upon her return to Fang, Namaari told Virana about Sisu. "She can fix what we broke," she said, feeling hopeful. "She can bring everyone back."

But Virana didn't share in Namaari's excitement. She believed once people came back to life, they would seek revenge on Fang, unless Fang had the dragon and the Gem shards.

But Namaari knew that Raya would not give up Sisu. So Virana vowed not to give Raya a choice.

Meanwhile, Raya, Sisu and their group were back together and gathered around a campfire. Tong and Boun argued over a simmering pot. "There's too much spice," Tong said.

"Uh, no, there's too much bamboo," said Boun.

Raya pulled palm sugar from her pouch.

"May I?" she asked. Using a trick her father had taught her, she carefully sprinkled it into the broth. The soup was delicious.

"Careful, Noi," Tong said, grabbing the baby, who was trying to fill her bowl with more soup. Everyone stared at him. "It's her name," he said. "It's written on her collar."

When a flare went up over the palace, Sisu asked, "What does that mean?"

"We're on," said Raya. She turned to Sisu. "Until we get that Gem and confirm Namaari's actually on our side, stay hidden."

Sisu nodded.

Moments later, Raya stepped out to meet Namaari by the shore. "I see you got my gift," said Raya, looking at the pendant.

"I never thought I'd see it again," said Namaari, and the two of them shared a smile. "So... did you bring it?"

Raya watched as Namaari set the Gem piece on the ground. She stared at it for a moment in disbelief.

Sisu stepped out – but Namaari lifted her crossbow!
"I'm taking Sisu and all the Gem pieces," Namaari shouted.
Raya and the group told Sisu to get back.
"You just want a better world. Like we all do," Sisu said.
"I trust you, Namaari."
When Raya saw Namaari hesitate, she made her move.

When Raya pulled out her sword, it
hit Namaari's crossbow and accidentally
released an arrow! It cut through the air,
striking Sisu.

The dragon fell into the canal and
disappeared underneath the water.

Shocked, Namaari dropped her crossbow, grabbed her Dragon Gem piece, and ran.

"SISU!" Raya screamed, running towards the fallen dragon.

As Raya prepared to jump in after her, the river magically disappeared.

"No dragons, no water," said Tong. "Now there is nothing to stop the Druun."

Across the empty riverbed, crowds of Druun emerged.

When the group looked around for Raya, she was gone.

Clutching her sword and a Gem piece, Raya marched into Fang. Fury pulsed through her veins as she searched for Namaari.

When Raya entered the throne room, she saw Namaari staring at her mother, who was now stone.

"Namaari!" shouted Raya.

"Let's finish this!" said Namaari, raising her weapon.

The two began to duel.

"I didn't mean for any of this to happen!" Namaari said. "I don't care if you believe me. Sisu did. But you didn't trust her. That's why we're here."

Raya hesitated.

"Do whatever you want," Namaari said, "but you're as much to blame for this as I am."

In that moment, Raya realised her rage had blinded her to what was going on around her. She raced off to help her friends.

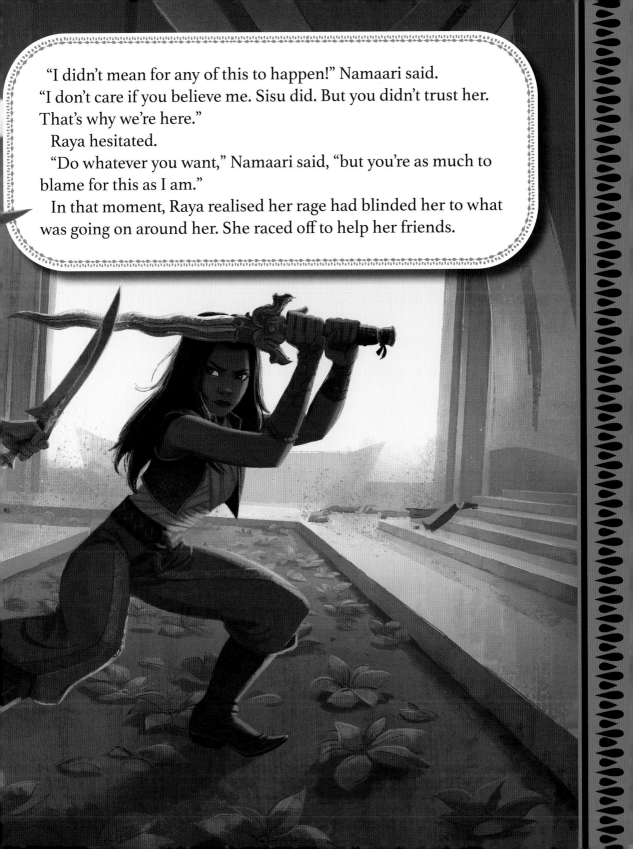

Meanwhile, with Druun closing in around them, Tong, Boun and the others raced into Fang and split up, each taking a Gem shard. They bravely battled against the Druun, helping the people of Fang escape to safety. Even Namaari joined in the fight.

Suddenly, an earthquake caused the surrounding buildings to topple, trapping the group and leaving them no way to escape. The Druun edged ever closer. When Tong saw Namaari, he wanted revenge for what had been done to Sisu.

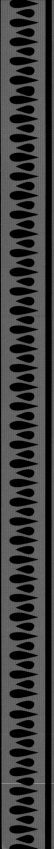

With no options left, Raya could finally see what they had to do. "We have to come together and fix this." She handed Namaari her Gem piece and stepped away.

A Druun passed through Raya, turning her to stone! Following Raya's lead, Boun, Tong and the others each handed Namaari their Gem piece. One by one, the Druun turned them to stone.

Namaari stood, shocked and confused, holding the pieces. But when she saw Raya's face, frozen in stone, she knew what she had to do.

She assembled the pieces and placed her hand on Raya's shoulder. A Druun washed over her and she too was turned to stone.

The Gem's light went out.

But slowly, a tiny pulse of light returned and grew until... BOOM! The Druun disappeared!

Droplets of glowing rain began to fall, melting the stone that covered the people, bringing them back to life! They had done it! The Druun were defeated and the world had been saved.

Meanwhile, in the dry river bed, water rose from the ground and soon there was a powerful river flowing once more. A glowing light rose up out of the river, growing brighter until Sisu burst out! She ran on raindrops, across the sky, with her siblings, overjoyed to see them again.

"Raya," said Sisu, landing beside her. "I. Am. So hungry!"

"I got some jerky?"

"Not that hungry!"

The friends smiled and hugged tightly.

Raya and Tuk Tuk hurried back to Heart. As they reached the bridge, stood in front of them was Raya's father, Benja. Raya rushed to him and the two hugged tighter than they ever had before.

Raya introduced her father to Sisu and the rest of her new friends.

"Father, welcome to... Kumandra," said Raya.